Put Beginning Readers on the Right Track with
ALL ABOARD READING™

The All Aboard Reading series is especially for beginning readers. Written by noted authors and illustrated in full color, these are books that children really and truly *want* to read—books to excite their imagination, tickle their funny bone, expand their interests, and support their feelings. With four different reading levels, All Aboard Reading lets you choose which books are most appropriate for your children and their growing abilities.

Picture Readers—for Ages 3 to 6
Picture Readers have super-simple texts, with many nouns appearing as rebus pictures. At the end of each book are 24 flash cards—on one side is the rebus picture; on the other side is the written-out word.

Level 1—for Preschool through First-Grade Children
Level 1 books have very few lines per page, very large type, easy words, lots of repetition, and pictures with visual "cues" to help children figure out the words on the page.

Level 2—for First-Grade to Third-Grade Children
Level 2 books are printed in slightly smaller type than Level 1 books. The stories are more complex, but there is still lots of repetition in the text, and many pictures. The sentences are quite simple and are broken up into short lines to make reading easier.

Level 3—for Second-Grade through Third-Grade Children
Level 3 books have considerably longer texts, harder words, and more complicated sentences.

All Aboard for happy reading!

To Boone: Now you're in a book, too—S.A.K.

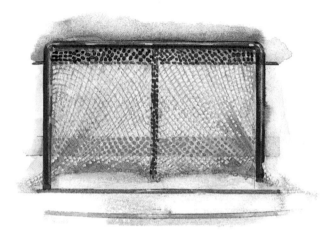

Photo credits: back cover, Brian Bahr/Allsport; p.15, Rick Stewart/Allsport; p.25, Craig Melvin/Allsport; p.35, Brian Bahr/Allsport; p.47, Steve Babineau/Allsport.

Kramer, Sydelle.
    In the cage : four goalie greats / by S.A. Kramer ; illustrated by Ken Call with photographs.
        p.   cm. — (All aboard reading. Level 3)
    Summary: Examines the careers and accomplishments of four superstar hockey goalkeepers: Dominik Hasek, Martin Brodeur, Patrick Roy, and Ed Belfour.
    1. Hockey goalkeepers Biography Juvenile literature. 2. Hockey Goalkeeping Juvenile literature. [1. Hockey players.] I. Call, Ken, ill. II. Title. III. Series.
    GV848.5.A1K736   1999
    796.96'0922—dc21
    [B]   99-26207
                                                                                                CIP
ISBN 0-448-42084-8 (GB)   A B C D E F G H I J
ISBN 0-448-42083-X (pbk.)   A B C D E F G H I J

ALL
ABOARD
READING™
Level 3
Grades 2-3

IN THE CAGE
FOUR GOALIE GREATS

By S.A. Kramer
Illustrated by Ken Call

With photographs

Grosset & Dunlap • New York

Medal Man

The Winter Olympics, February 20,
1998. It's shoot-out time in Big Hat
Arena, Nagano, Japan. Overtime has just
ended in the semifinal between the Czech
Republic and Canada. But the score is
still tied, 1-1. The winning team will skate
for the gold medal.

In a shoot-out, teams get five chances
to score. They take turns sending solo
shooters down the ice. Using all the tricks
they know, the shooters try to blast the
puck past the goalie. The man in the net
must have nerves of steel.

The Czechs are underdogs, but right now they feel confident. That's because their goalie is Dominik Hasek (you say it like this: HA-shek), the best in the NHL. Six-foot-one Dominik is usually between the posts for the Buffalo Sabres. But he's Czech, and in the Olympics, he plays for his country.

Experts everywhere agree that thirty-two-year-old Dominik is a great goalie. Nicknamed The Dominator, he has an unusual style of play. Double-jointed, he twists, bends, and stretches his body in all kinds of amazing ways. Dominik is so rubbery he can sit on the floor, spread his legs, and touch his stomach to the ground. One reporter calls him a "human Gumby."

During a game, he often seems to be out of position. Then he blocks the puck by rolling on the ice from one post to the other. Sometimes he nearly stands on his head to make a save.

But despite his talent, Dominik has a problem. He doesn't always control his feelings. In the 1997 playoffs, he had temper tantrums, even smashing his stick against the post. After one game, he fought with a reporter and grabbed him by the throat.

During the playoffs, Dominik took himself out of games. He had injured his right knee, but some people didn't believe the injury was that serious. Fans began to feel Dominik just couldn't take playoff pressure.

By the start of the 1997-98 season, he was in a real slump. The hometown crowd booed him loudly each time he was introduced. To drown the boos out, the Sabres played a tape of cheering fans. That didn't help much.

Dominik understood how the crowd felt. More than anything, he wanted to prove he could take the heat. He shook off his slow start, tying the NHL record of six shutouts in one month. Then he sparked his team in the Olympics. Now, with the semifinal game on the line, he has to stop the best players in the world.

The Czechs score first. Dominik must protect their lead. He stops the first Canadian shot with his right shoulder. With his glove, he tips the second one over the net. The third goes wide.

The fourth Canadian shooter fakes right, then skates left. Dominik's in trouble—the shooter has fooled him. Losing his stick, he plops on his back. It looks like the Canadians are going to score.

But Dominik won't give up. From the ice he cranes his neck and catches sight of the puck. With his legs in the air, he sticks his glove up. The shot slams wide off the post. It's a miracle save!

The fifth shooter fakes too, but
Dominik is ready. He moves in front of
the Canadian, and the shot misses.

The Czechs win, 2-1! Dominik bends
down and kisses the ice. Then he starts
throwing off his equipment. His
teammates rush from the bench, piling
on top of him.

Dominik's overjoyed. He's shown he
can win the big game. The shoot-out,

he says, was "unbelievable pressure, the biggest pressure of my life."

The Czechs go on to win the gold medal. Dominik has a shutout in the game. In his country he's a hero. He is to NHL fans, too. When he returns to Buffalo, a cheering crowd greets him at the airport. A mob of kids surrounds his house to congratulate him.

By the end of the 1998 NHL season, Dominik's in the record books. He's the first goalie ever to be named Most Valuable Player twice. The trophy for best goalie goes to him for the fourth time.

Dominik's getting used to winning awards. Yet hockey didn't always come easy to him. When he was five, he had problems with his back. "I didn't walk the right way," he says. "My back was bent." Every morning until he was eight, he did special exercises to straighten his spine. Dominik says those exercises help him even today.

When he was old enough for hockey, there was no one to help him. Few coaches knew how to teach kids to play goalie. His father, a miner, was home only on the weekends. His mother didn't like the sport—she wanted Dominik to get a good education.

But Dominik was determined. He watched other goalies and imitated them. Despite his lack of training, he played for local teams. For nine years, he was a star in the Czech league. At the same time, he studied to be a history teacher.

In 1990, the NHL's Chicago Blackhawks asked him to join them. Dominik couldn't resist, even though he didn't understand any English at the time.

It turned out the Blackhawks didn't know much about Dominik. The coach disapproved of his playing style. One man said "he flopped around the ice like some fish." Dominik was sent to the minors. He didn't get much NHL playing time until he was traded to the Sabres in 1992.

Now he's led the league in save percentage five years in a row. He once blocked 70 shots in a playoff game for a 1-0 win. Experts all agree that Dominik has become the best hockey goalie in the world.

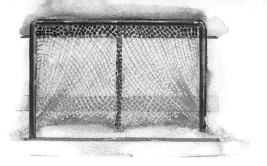

Dreamer

New Jersey, April 17, 1997. It looks as if the Devils will beat the Montreal Canadiens in the playoff opener. The score's 4-2, and there's less than a minute left in the game. But the Canadiens won't give up. They send their goalie from the net for an extra shooter. It's up to Martin Brodeur to protect the Devils' lead.

Twenty-four years old, Martin is the NHL's best young goalie. The 1994 Rookie of the Year, he helped the Devils win the 1995 Stanley Cup in just his second season. He is always calm and confident between the posts. During breaks in the action, he skates in circles, takes deep breaths, and winks at friends in the stands.

Martin is happy being a goalie. But his teammates know he has a secret dream. A great puckhandler, he's always wanted to score a goal.

For years, Martin has practiced a special shot. Outside the net, he reaches back with his stick and swings. The puck soars down the rink like a golf ball. If he's hit it just right, it goes into the opposite goal.

But Martin knows he needs more than practice to score. He needs luck. Only one goalie in NHL playoff history has managed this feat.

Tonight, though, Martin isn't thinking about scoring. He just wants to play his best. That's because he's a Montreal boy, up against his hometown team. In fact, Martin's dad, who was an Olympic goalie, is the Canadiens' team photographer.

Now the puck is loose to the right of

the Devils' cage. Martin gets his stick on it and skates around the net. He sees a Canadien charge directly at him—he's got to act fast to clear the puck. If he can't, the Canadiens could get a quick goal and still have time to tie.

By the left post, Martin swings his stick with all his might. He socks the puck over the heads of all the players. It flies through the air, hits the ice, and slides toward the end of the rink. With no one to stop it, it just keeps sliding—into the Canadiens' net!

Martin's scored a goal from 178 feet away. He can hardly believe it—his dream has come true. Scoring, he later says, is "the greatest thing that happened to me."

The crowd of 19,040 leaps up cheering. Martin jumps high into the air, then starts to laugh. One of his teammates skates over and hops into his arms. The rest of the Devils swarm around him with their congratulations.

This isn't the first time Martin has earned a place in the record books. In 1995-96, he set the NHL record for most minutes ever played—4,433. In the next season he allowed only 1.88 goals a game, the league's lowest average in twenty-five years. He also had 10 shutouts, the most in twenty years.

No one who knows Martin is surprised by his feats. He's been in love with the game since he was three. That's when his dad first took him to the Canadiens' arena. As he stood atop the net, his dad snapped his picture. Martin was thrilled.

At five, he was a goalie. But he was the youngest kid on his team at seven, and didn't get much of a chance to play. Then the starting goalie got hurt and Martin took over. The coach was so impressed he asked Martin to stay.

Martin had a special talent. He also had a special view of the game—an insider's view. By the time he was a teenager, he was working as his father's assistant. Behind the scenes at the arena, he watched the Canadiens practice. His father introduced him to the athletes, telling them his son would one day be in the NHL too.

When Martin was fourteen, he didn't seem special anymore. His team suddenly dropped him. Shocked and upset, Martin wanted to quit hockey. But his older brother told him, "You go back and play." Martin says, "If he hadn't, I might not be here now."

Martin kept practicing—and won back his position. He went on to play three years of junior hockey and one full year in the minors. When he was just nineteen, he made it to the NHL and the Devils.

At six feet one, 205 pounds, Martin seemed to fill the whole net. A patient guy, he always waited for the shooter to make the first move. Then he took just the right position to block the puck and prevent rebounds.

He always worked hard. One of the first on the ice in practice, Martin was one of the last to leave. Often, he took extra practice. It paid off. In 1997-98, he allowed 1.89 goals a game and had 10 shutouts.

Martin's a guy who's had all his hockey dreams come true. But he's never let success go to his head. When he visits Montreal, he plays street hockey with old friends. Kids sometimes come to his home and ask him to play with them— and he does.

Off the ice Martin is easygoing and friendly. He's popular with both teammates and fans. They can tell he's someone who enjoys his job. Martin says, "I love to be in goal, to be the last line of defense, to be all alone."

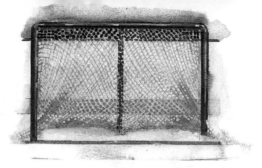

Mr. Clutch

June 8, 1996. It's raining rats in Miami, Florida. Colorado Avalanche goalie Patrick Roy (you say it like this: WAH) knows he's in trouble now. He's watching Florida Panther fans go wild as they hurl big toy plastic rats at him. That's what they always do to an opposing goalie when their team scores.

Patrick's just allowed a goal in the third game of the Stanley Cup finals. The Avalanche lead the series, 2-0, but the Panthers are fighting back.

It's only the first period, but the game has to stop as the rats come pouring down. Other goalies usually take shelter in their nets. Not Patrick. He stands boldly in the crease as hundreds of the toys fly through the air. "I've got too much pride to hide," he says.

That's not surprising. Patrick has always been a spunky guy. Everyone in hockey knows he never shies away from a fight. He even teases opposing players. Once he winked at an opponent after he blocked his shot.

Thirty-year-old Patrick certainly has his own way of playing the game. Before each start, he writes his children's names on his stick. He makes sure "Be a Warrior" is printed under one of his pads.

When he takes the ice, he skates halfway to the blue line, turns, and stares at the net. "I'm imagining the net shrinking," he says, so that it will be harder for opponents to score.

During a game, Patrick does things no other goalie would. He talks to the goalposts. He never skates on a line, stepping over it instead. Whenever there's a break, he tosses his head, cranes his neck, and shrugs his shoulders. It looks like he's gone crazy, but he's just trying to cool off under his hot mask.

Ever confident, Patrick thinks for himself. He uses the butterfly style, even though some experts criticize him for it. That means he spreads his legs wide, then falls to his knees to block a shot. As though he's riding a pogo stick, he pops back up an instant later.

Most young NHL goalies say Patrick is their model. They admire his quick glove hand, and even quicker reflexes. When a

shooter fires low, Patrick is always in the perfect spot to block the puck. At 6 feet, 190 pounds, he stops the high shots with his glove or shoulders.

Patrick's teammates admire him too. His fighting spirit has made him a club leader. "I hate to lose," he says, so he plays all out. One teammate reports, "When Patrick Roy says we're going to win, you stop worrying."

But now Panther fans are hoping to shake Patrick up. They keep pounding him with rat after rat. Two hundred of the toys strike his body. Even more lie scattered around him on the ice.

Patrick shrugs the attack off. But when

the action begins again, he decides to shut the Panthers down. For the next 153 minutes, he stops every one of their shots. The rain of rats has just made him more determined to win.

The Avalanche take Game 3. In Game 4 Patrick holds the Panthers scoreless with 63 saves. After five hours, his team wins, 1-0, in triple overtime. Thanks to

Patrick, it's an Avalanche sweep, and the longest scoreless game in Stanley Cup history.

Patrick has made sure his team has won its first championship ever. As always, he's been in top form in the clutch. One player calls him "the best pressure goaltender in the history of the league."

Ever since he was seven, Patrick has wanted to be a goalie. As a boy in Montreal, Canada, he'd tie pillows to his legs with belts because he didn't have real pads. When an NHL pro gave young Patrick a stick, the boy was so thrilled, he slept with it each night.

By the time he was a teenager, Patrick was a star in junior hockey. His grandmother was his biggest fan,

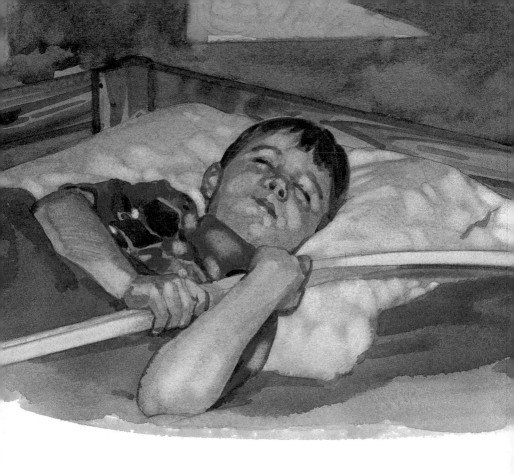

encouraging him to become a pro. He
was only twenty when he made it to the
NHL in 1985.

Patrick played for his hometown
team, the Canadiens. Those were the
days when he ate only fries, potato
chips, and junk food. His eating habits

didn't stop him from winning. In 1986, Patrick was named the youngest playoff MVP ever.

In Montreal, Patrick was a hero. Young girls would chase after him and try to rip his shirt off. Fans nicknamed him Saint Patrick as he and the Canadiens won two Stanley Cups. Three times he was named best goalie of the year.

But by 1995, things were going wrong for Patrick. He was playing badly. Then he had a fight with his coach. After demanding a trade, he went to the Avalanche. Colorado fans were delighted, and Patrick didn't disappoint them. He became only the fifth goalie in NHL history to win more than 400 games.

Patrick just keeps on winning. He holds the NHL record for most playoff victories ever. He's also made the most playoff appearances. He's one of only two goalies to ever win the playoff MVP twice. It's no wonder his coach calls him "the greatest goalie in Stanley Cup history."

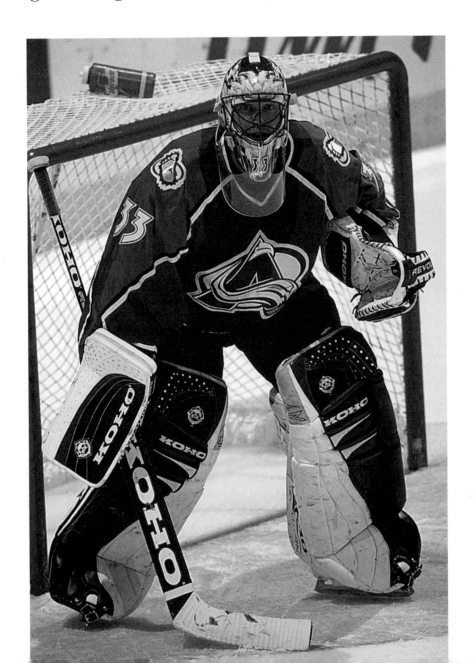

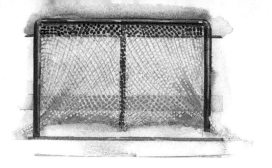

Rink Rat

It's the winter of 1977 in Carman,
Manitoba, Canada. Twelve-year-old Ed
Belfour is freezing. He's playing hockey
in an indoor rink, but the temperature's
still below zero. That's not unusual in
Carman. It's a small farm town where the
winters are long and hard. It stays so cold
outside, the rink never seems to heat up
at all.

Ed has a technique for trying to stay
warm. He doesn't sit on the bench when
he's not in the game—he goes right to
the dressing room. Between periods, he
takes off his skates and hops around in

his socks. That's the way he gets the blood back in his toes.

Ed's glad he's not the goalie. He knows the guy in the cage gets the coldest. Besides, Ed's favorite position is center. He loves to skate fast and score, and check opponents hard.

Ed's been crazy about hockey ever since he was five. That's when he got his first pair of skates. He calls himself a "rink rat."

When Ed was six, he tried playing goalie for his team. He loved the equipment, but staying in the net was hard for him. Guarding the goal didn't compare to shooting and scoring. And standing around between the pipes got him icy cold.

Still, every now and then, his coach put him in the net. And at twelve, he's become the team's backup goalie.

Most of the time, Ed's a strong, tough center. But sometimes he goes after the puck so hard, he doesn't skate a clean game. Even worse, he may lose his temper if a play goes wrong. Unlike most of his teammates, he spends a lot of time in the penalty box. More and more, his coach has gotten annoyed with him.

Today the coach makes a decision. He doesn't care how cold netminding gets or

how much Ed wants to play center.
"You're playing goal," he orders.
Between the posts, Ed will get into less
trouble.

Ed knows he isn't very good at his new
position. For three long years he works
hard to improve, since it's the only way he
gets to play. At fifteen, he tries out for his
high school team.

Ed doesn't make the team. It's a terrible
shock. He feels so crushed, he thinks
about giving up the sport for good. But
the next year he gets lucky. There's a new
coach and he gives Ed a chance.

It's late in the high school season when
Ed gets a really big break. His team is
down in the championship playoffs. A
desperate coach asks Ed to come in off
the bench. Ed hasn't played in a while—
but he wins two games!

Now he's on his way. He doesn't think about playing center anymore. In his first year at the University of North Dakota, he becomes a star goalie. Losing only four games, he helps his team win the 1987 NCAA (National Collegiate Athletic Association) crown. The NHL's Chicago Blackhawks decide they want him.

Ed spends two years in the minors before joining the team. Then, in 1990-91, he has one of the greatest rookie seasons ever. The boy who hated being in the cage wins more games than any goalie in Blackhawks history. He's named Rookie of the Year, leads the NHL in save percentage, and wins the league's award for best

goaltender. Ed's the only NHL rookie goalie ever to accomplish all that.

Still, he doesn't take his stardom for granted. Each game is important to him. On the days he takes the ice, he thinks only about hockey. He won't see or talk to anyone. His equipment must "be perfect," he says, so he examines it carefully. He even sharpens his own skate blades.

During a game, Ed crouches low and moves far out into the crease. Instead of his glove or his stick, he'll often use his five-foot-eleven body to block the puck. Just like an acrobat, he'll throw himself around on the ice. He handles the puck so well, one reporter calls him "a third defenseman."

The very next year, Ed again wins the award for best goalie. He becomes one of only five netminders to ever have two seasons with 40 or more wins. Fans in Chicago start chanting "Eddie! Eddie!" every time he makes a save.

No matter how many players crowd near the crease, Ed always seems to pick up the puck. Because of his sharp eyesight, he's called The Eagle. Ed's proud of his nickname. He has a colorful picture of the bird painted on his mask.

He says, "The eagle...represents strength, excellent vision, and strong leadership."

Ed's nickname fits him when he's off the ice, too. He spends a lot of time in the air, flying his own plane. Even on the ground, he can't stay still. He drag races at speeds of 165 miles per hour, runs, bikes, and swims.

In 1997-98, Ed joins the Dallas Stars. He immediately sets a Stars record for shutouts and wins. That year he leads the NHL in goals against average. In 1998-99, the Stars win the Stanley Cup. Ed's strong goaltending is one of the keys to their victory.

Once the boy who wanted to play center, Ed is now a dedicated goalie. But the change in his position didn't end his temper tantrums. Ed will fight not just with opponents but also with coaches. If teammates hit practice shots too close to him, he'll go after them. One reporter calls him Crazy Eddie.

Ed's the first to admit he's an emotional player. "It's just my will to win, to be the best," he says. Ed's wife reports, "He has to win even at home in Scrabble."

Ed's come a long way since his coach forced him to be a goalie. He never gave up on the game, even when he had to struggle just to get on the team. His determination made him a star.

Then in 1998-1999, one of Ed's lifelong dreams comes true. The Stars win the Stanley Cup. Ed's strong goaltending is one of the keys to victory. In the sixth and deciding game, he has fifty-three saves in triple overtime. He says later, "I was getting a real good bead on the puck...I felt in the zone."

The Stars win that game 2-1 over the Buffalo Sabres. Afterwards, a proud Ed skates around the rink holding the Stanley Cup high. "I can't describe the rush I got," he tells the fans. "I didn't want to put it down."